CITY

WRECKING VALENTINE'S DAY!

By Trey King

Illustrated by Sean Wang

SCHOLASTIC INC.

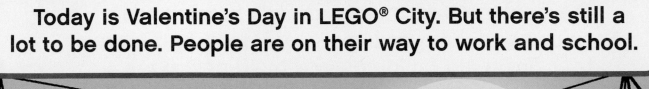

Today is Valentine's Day in LEGO® City. But there's still a lot to be done. People are on their way to work and school.

The construction crew is already hard at work. They use wrecking ball trucks, tractors, and trailers to tear down old buildings and build new ones.

CRASH!

Nearby, a scientist is also up early working. She is mixing different chemicals in her lab.

"Uh-oh. That doesn't look good," the scientist says.
The strange pink mist goes out the open window. It
floats down over the construction site next door.

When the foreman comes back, he is ready to work . . .

One of the construction workers is protecting the wrecking ball. "We can't swing it into the building! It might get hurt," he says.

Another construction worker is trying to charm his tractor. "You're the most beautiful tractor I've ever seen," he tells it.

"Hey, that's *my* letter!" one of the construction workers cries.

"You can't have it!" the mailman shouts back. "I'm in love with the mail!"

Another worker suddenly loves the portable toilet.
"No one can use this toilet. It's mine!" he says.

"This is crazy!" the foreman says. "Everyone is suddenly in love. I need to figure out what happened before things get any worse . . ."

But things *do* get worse. The wind blows the strange pink cloud over the town square. Luckily, the foreman sees the pink cloud coming from the Science Lab. "I need to get there, and fast!"

Now the whole city is acting strangely! The scientist's pink cloud has made *everyone* fall in love! Cats are chasing dogs. A grandma asks a wrestler to marry her. Even a policeman asks a crook to be his valentine.

"Excuse me," the foreman says. "Do you know what happened outside?"

"I do. It's my cat's fault. Mister Kitty accidentally made a love potion," the scientist says. "But I think I can fix it."

The foreman helps the scientist make up a cure in her lab.

"We did it," the scientist says. "But how do we get it to everybody?"

"I think I can help with that!" the foreman says.

The foreman calls his cousin—a police helicopter pilot. The three heroes fly over the city and spray the cure over everyone who is crazy in love.

Soon, everyone is back to normal.
"I'm sorry about the accident," says the scientist.
"Accidents happen," the foreman says. "But the important thing is that no one was hurt. And we worked together to fix it."

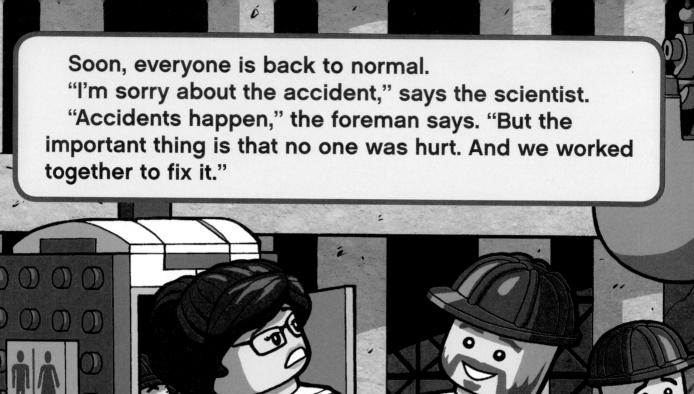

"What a crazy morning!" says one construction worker. "You've got that right," the foreman says. "Now, I'd *love* for you to get back to work!"

23